Jack Outwits the Giants

Jack Outwits the Giants

adapted and illustrated
by Paul Brett Johnson

MARGARET K. McELDERRY BOOKS

New York London Toronto Sydney Singapore

ONE TIME JACK was off on a journey when all of a sudden it blew up a big, dark storm. Before Jack could find cover, the sky was pouring out a waterfall.

Directly a slice of lightning lit up the valley and Jack caught sight of a farmhouse off in the distance. He slogged his way to the farmhouse and pounded on the door. It was answered by a big giant-woman, tall as a barn loft.

"Lord, child! You look like a drownded cat. Get in
here and dry off by the fire."

The giant-woman rattled around in the kitchen and came
back with some hot coffee and cornmeal mush.

"Here, this ought to warm your innards. What do they call
you, son?"

"Name's Jack."

"Well, Jack, you just make yourself to home. My husband'll be
back any minute. He'll sure want to make your acquaintance."

It wasn't long till Jack heard a stomping on the front porch that
shook the whole house. The door banged open and in stepped the
biggest, wildest-looking human being Jack ever did see. That big
giant-man had *two heads,* both of 'em mud-fence ugly! Jack had a
notion to run back out in the storm fast as he could, but the giant-
man was in the way.

"What's for supper, ol' woman?" the giant-man bellowed.

"Cornmeal mush."

"*Cornmeal mush. Cornmeal mush.* That's all you ever fix!"

"Hush your gripin', ol' man, and say howdy to tender young Jack, here."

Both of that giant-man's heads looked right at Jack. They gave Jack a sniff. "Well, Jack, that storm ain't about to let up, so you might as well stay the night. They's a nice dry pallet in the loft. We'll wake you for breakfast."

Jack suspicioned that wouldn't be all they'd do for breakfast, but he made a show of stretching and yawning anyway. "Thank you kindly, mister. Reckon I'll take you up on your offer."

Jack had no sooner climbed the ladder to the loft than he heard a loud raspy sound. At first he thought it was the wind whipping and howling through the trees. But then he figured out it was coming from directly below. Jack peeped down. Them two giants had all three heads together stirring up misery!

Now, to a giant a whisper is a whisper, but to a regular feller it might as well be a hog call. *Sounds like the chances of me keeping my hide are getting mighty slim,* thought Jack. *I better do something.* He looked around the loft till he spied a big sack of feed in the corner. He lugged it over to the pallet and plumped it up under the covers to make it look like somebody was sound asleep. Then Jack hid behind the chimney.

'Long about midnight here come that ol' giant-man
clomp-clomp-clomping up the ladder. He poked one
head in the loft and looked around. Then he poked in
the other head.

The giant-man had a big club. He went over to the pallet and commenced pounding that sack of feed with it. "I'll have me a fine Jack breakfast come morning," he said. When the giant-man was satisfied he had finished off Jack, he clomp-clomp-clomped back down the ladder.

The next morning Jack
scurried down, keen as a
sapling. Both of that giant-
man's mouths dropped wide
open and the giant-woman looked
like she had just seen a haint.

"Didn't have no trouble sleeping
last night?" asked the giant-man.

"Come to think on it, 'round
midnight there was a swarm of gnats
that got to pesterin' me. Otherwise I slept
just fine." Jack made a big stretch. "Well,
guess I better be gettin' along. I appreciate
the hospitality."

"Hold it right there, boy. You ain't going nowheres. I got cornmeal mush coming outta my ears, and I'm craving some meat for breakfast."

"Be careful!" the giant-woman warned. "That boy's been witched, else he wouldn't be drawin' air this very minute."

The giant-man rubbed first one chin and then the other. "Well, young Jack, if you been witched you'll have to prove it. They's five milk-cows up in the pasture. I want you to carry 'em all down here on your back and milk 'em. Anybody that's been witched ought to be able to do a little chore like that. If you can't, then I'm going to eat you for breakfast."

"Easy as pie," said Jack. He headed for the pasture, but he was mighty worried. "I can't carry *one* cow, let alone *five!*"

Just then Jack noticed a patch of milkweed growing by the fencerow and he got an idea. He ambled over, plucked a few milkweed pods, and snuck 'em in his pocket.

"Hey, Mister Giant-man! I got a better idea," Jack
hollered. "It's too much trouble to go way up to the
pasture. If it's all the same to you, I'll just milk a few of
these rocks layin' around the front yard."

"That's about the foolishest notion I ever did hear!"
said the giant-man.

Jack didn't pay him no mind. Just bent over and acted
like he was picking up a rock. At the same time he
pulled a milkweed pod out of his pocket. Jack
held out his fist, squinched his eyes, and
gritted his teeth. Lo and behold a line of
milk started dripping down!

"*How'd you do that?*" asked the
giant-man.

"Easy as pie," said Jack, and
he did it again.

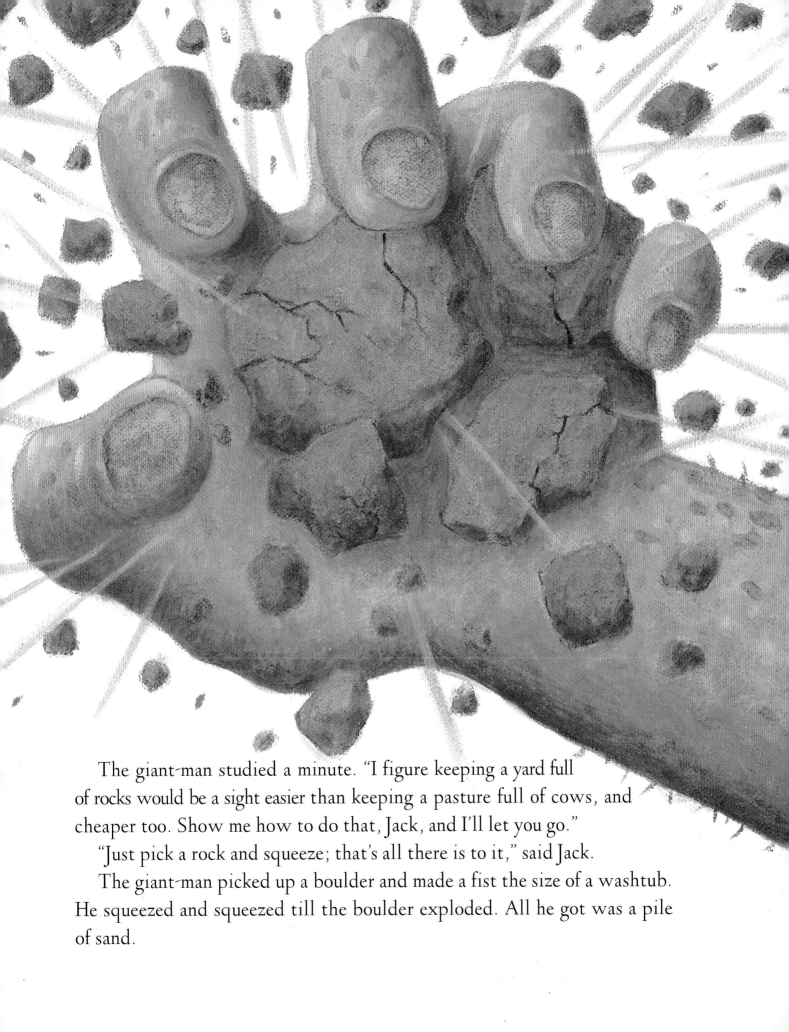

The giant-man studied a minute. "I figure keeping a yard full
of rocks would be a sight easier than keeping a pasture full of cows, and
cheaper too. Show me how to do that, Jack, and I'll let you go."

"Just pick a rock and squeeze; that's all there is to it," said Jack.

The giant-man picked up a boulder and made a fist the size of a washtub.
He squeezed and squeezed till the boulder exploded. All he got was a pile
of sand.

"Reckon the hard part is choosing
'twixt a milking rock and a plain one?" asked the giant-woman.

"Might be," said the giant-man. "Might be. But I'm still hankerin' for some
breakfast meat. I got another test for you, Jack. Go on down to the creek and bring up
a bucket of wash water. If you can't do it, then you're as good as in the frying pan."

"Easy as pie," said Jack. But when he got to the creek his eyes shot open like
window shades. The water bucket was nigh big as a henhouse. Why, he couldn't
budge that bucket with it empty!

Jack figured a bit, then rolled up his shirt sleeves and his britchy-legs. He waded out to the middle of the creek and started feeling around for something.

"What're you up to, boy?" hollered the giant-man.

"Just looking for a good handhold, that's all."

"What for?" asked the giant-woman.

"Thought I'd save y'all a bunch of trouble. Thought I'd just carry the creek up there so you wouldn't have to walk so far for wash water."

"Lord-a-mercy! Don't you bring that creek up here!" squalled the giant-woman. "Next good rain, it'll flood the cornfield."

"Well, if you won't let me carry the creek up there, I'm sure not going to fool with one little ol' bucket of water," said Jack.

"All right, then. Forget about the wash water and just let the creek be. Come on back up here," said the giant-man.

It looked like the giant-man was just about ready to let Jack go, but then his belly got to growling like a sawmill. "Jack, you sure would taste awful good fried up cracklin'-brown. You're gonna have to do one more thing. See that big oak tree yonder? Heave it up by the roots, haul it over here, and chop it for firewood. Otherwise you'll be greasing my mustaches."

The oak tree must've been three hundred years old, big around as a silo! "Well, Mister Giant-man," said Jack, "I reckon you got me this time. Go ahead, poke up the fire and grease the skillet."

The giant-man started drooling just to hear Jack talk that-a-way.

"Too bad you won't have time to eat me, though," said Jack.

"You're plumb foolish, boy! I got the whole day to chew you up, little at a time so's to make it last."

"If I was you, I'd chew fast," said Jack. "I reckon you know they's a bounty out for you and your wife. I just left the sheriff yesterday. 'If I ain't back by morning,' I told him, 'you and the posse come a-looking!' They ought to be along any time, now."

The giant-woman started wailing and carrying on. "I told you we shouldn't of eat them two deputies. Now we're in for it!"

"Hush up, woman, and let me think," the giant-man snarled.

Jack cupped one ear. "Hear that? Must be a hundred or more coming on horseback!"

By now the giant-woman was screaming and running in circles. Her two-headed husband just stood there in puzzlement.

"Tell you what. Y'all were good enough to take me in out of the rain, so I'm going to return the favor. You go hide in that well over yonder and when the sheriff and his posse get here I'll tell 'em you fled the territory."

The pair of giants didn't waste a minute. They grabbed hold of the rope and let themselves down into the well.

"Don't make a sound," Jack warned. "I hear the posse riding up the holler right now!"

No sooner had the giants dropped out of sight than Jack kicked up the awfullest ruckus you ever heard. KA-WHACK! KA-BOOM! He rattled dishpans and banged lard buckets. He busted up chairs and beat on fence rails.

"Howdy, Sheriff!" Jack yelled. "No, I ain't seen hide nor hair of them giants. They must of heard you coming. I bet they're outta the territory by now. All right, see you later."

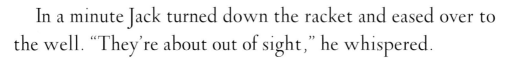

In a minute Jack turned down the racket and eased over to the well. "They're about out of sight," he whispered.

"Is it safe to come out?" asked the giant-woman.

"No, not yet. Wait till I count to three."

Jack looked around and found a sharp axe. "ONE!"

Jack sighted the rope and drew back the axe. "TWO!"

"We're on the way up," said the giant-man.

"THREE!"

You know, a regular well only runs so deep, but they say a giant's well hasn't got a bottom to it. That pair of giants is still falling, like as not.

AUTHOR'S NOTE

When European settlers came to America in the eighteenth century, they brought their fairy tales with them—including those about a boy-hero named Jack. The stories that have since become known as "Jack Tales" are mostly Appalachian versions.

Whether back in Europe or right here in the American South, Jack always seems to find himself in challenging situations. Often he meets up with unsavory characters. Depending on who is doing the telling, Jack can be lazy or industrious, dull or crafty. But he is never so lazy or so dull that he can't outwit a hungry giant!

—P. B. J.
Lexington, Kentucky

For my "invisible" friends—they know who they are.

Margaret K. McElderry Books
An imprint of Simon & Schuster Children's Publishing Division
1230 Avenue of the Americas
New York, New York 10020
Copyright © 2002 by Paul Brett Johnson
The text of this book is set in Deepdene.
The illustrations are rendered in acrylic paint on canvas.
Printed in Hong Kong
2 4 6 8 10 9 7 5 3
Library of Congress Cataloging-in-Publication Data
Johnson, Paul Brett.
Jack outwits the giants / adapted and illustrated by Paul Brett Johnson.
p. cm.
Summary: In this Appalachian folktale, Jack outwits two giants who want fresh meat for breakfast.
ISBN 0-689-83902-2
[1. Folklore—Appalachian Region.] I. Title.
PZ8.1.J635 Jac 2002
398.2'0974'02—dc21
[E]
2001030811